Produced by Ladybird Books Ltd
© 1995 Disney Enterprises, Inc.
1 3 5 7 9 10 8 6 4 2

DISNEY

The Jungle Book

MOUSE WORKS

Deep in the jungle, Bagheera the
panther was out hunting. Suddenly,
he heard a strange crying sound
coming from the river.

He went to find out what it was and
discovered a basket with a tiny baby
boy inside. "Why, it's a Man-cub!"
he said. "This little fellow needs
food and a mother's care. Perhaps
Mother Wolf will look after him."

Mother Wolf agreed to help. They
named the Man-cub Mowgli and he
grew up safe and happy in the jungle.

But everything changed when Mowgli was ten years old. Shere Khan, the man-eating tiger, heard about the Man-cub and came searching for him.

The wolves held an urgent meeting to discuss Mowgli's future. They agreed that Bagheera should take the boy back to the Man-village where he would be safe.

The next morning, Bagheera and
Mowgli set off on their long journey.
Mowgli was angry and upset. He
didn't understand why he had to
leave the jungle—it was his home!

When darkness fell, Bagheera and
Mowgli climbed a tree and settled
down to sleep on a branch.

Nearby, hiding under some leaves,
was Kaa, the python.

As soon as Bagheera was asleep, Kaa
slithered towards the Man-cub.

Kaa's shining yellow eyes seemed to have a magic power. Mowgli quickly fell under their spell and began to sink into a deep trance. Kaa started to slowly wind himself around the boy, ready to swallow him up!

Suddenly, Bagheera woke up and sprang at Kaa. He slapped the snake with his paw and sent him slithering away into the jungle.

At dawn, Mowgli was awakened by a very loud noise. He looked down from the tree and saw an old elephant marching through the jungle. His trunk was held high in the air.

"Up, two, three, four! Up, two, three, four!" the elephant trumpeted. Behind him, there were other elephants trying to keep up. It was Colonel Hathi and the Dawn Patrol.

13

Mowgli quickly leapt down from the tree to join them. The Man-cub was soon down on all fours, following a baby elephant. He had great fun trying to copy everything the little elephant did!

Eventually, Bagheera caught up with Mowgli. He wanted to continue their journey towards the Man-village. But Mowgli refused to go. He grabbed hold of a tree trunk and held on tightly.

Frustrated, Bagheera went off on his own, leaving the Man-cub by himself.

But not for long! As Mowgli wandered through the jungle he met a friendly bear called Baloo.

"Well now, what have we here?" Baloo asked. Mowgli introduced himself. He told Baloo how much he wanted to stay in the jungle. "No problem!" Baloo said, "I'll look after you!"

Baloo enjoyed teaching, and playing with, his new friend. Soon, Mowgli could fight like a bear, growl like a bear and even scratch like a bear!

Later that afternoon, Mowgli and
Baloo waded into the river to cool
off. As they gently floated along,
Mowgli sat on Baloo's tummy. It was
very peaceful and Baloo soon fell
fast asleep.

But watching from some trees was a
group of monkeys who were lying in
wait to kidnap Mowgli.

Suddenly, the monkeys sprang out from their hiding place and grabbed the Man-cub. "Hey! Let go of me!" Mowgli shouted.

When Baloo finally awoke, it was too late! The monkeys were already carrying Mowgli off to the ruined temple where they lived.

Luckily, Bagheera heard Mowgli's
cries and rushed to the river to help.
He found Baloo, who explained
what had happened. "We need a
rescue plan," Bagheera said...

Meanwhile, the monkeys had carried Mowgli back to the ruined temple, where their king, Louie, was sitting on his throne awaiting them.

"So, you're here at last!" Louie cried, as Mowgli was dropped beside him.

Louie offered to help Mowgli stay in the jungle. In return, he wanted to learn the secret of Man's red fire.

"Once I am the master of fire, I will be human just like you," Louie said. Before Mowgli could explain that he didn't know the secret, Louie declared that they would have a great feast in honor of their guest.

King Louie leapt from his throne.
He started to sing and dance as a
monkey beat out the rhythm on a
nearby tree trunk. As Mowgli's feet
began to tap to the music, he forgot
his troubles and joined in the fun.

Meanwhile, Baloo and Bagheera had reached the temple. They watched Mowgli and the monkeys from behind a wall.

"Baloo," whispered Bagheera. "You try and distract the monkeys while I rescue Mowgli."

Baloo had an idea…He dressed in some coconut shells and leaves to try and look like a lady ape. Then he waved at Louie.

The King thought the lady ape was very beautiful and rushed over to ask her to dance. He had no idea that it was really Baloo in disguise!

But as Baloo danced, his disguise
began to fall off. The angry monkeys
realised they had been tricked and
started to attack him.

Just as Bagheera rushed over to help, Baloo knocked over a pillar. The temple came crashing down. Luckily, Baloo and Bagheera managed to drag Mowgli to safety. The three friends ran deep into the jungle and found a place to rest.

That night, Bagheera and Baloo kept watch over Mowgli as he slept. It was time to discuss their young friend's future...

"The Man-cub *must* go to the Man-village," said Bagheera. "It's not safe for him to stay in the jungle."

Baloo finally had to admit that Bagheera was right.

So, the next morning, Baloo led Mowgli off towards the Man-village.

When the Man-cub found out where they were headed, he was very angry. "You don't want me to stay— you're just like Bagheera!" he shouted. Before Baloo could explain, Mowgli ran off into the jungle.

When Bagheera heard Mowgli had run away, he went to see Colonel Hathi and the Dawn Patrol.

"We need your help," Bagheera told him. "The Man-cub is alone in the jungle. We must find him before Shere Khan does."

At that very moment, close by, Shere Khan was stalking a deer. As he stopped and listened to Bagheera, he licked his lips. "The Man-cub is lost in the jungle, eh? I think I'll do everyone a good deed and find him first," he said. And off he went to begin his search.

It wasn't long before Shere Khan
spotted Mowgli in the distance.
Emerging from the shadows, the
tiger gave a roar. He leapt at Mowgli,
taking the Man-cub by surprise.

But Shere Khan stopped in mid-leap
and crashed to the ground—Baloo
had caught him by the tail!

Shere Khan roared with rage as he dragged Baloo behind him, but the brave bear was determined not to let go.

Eventually, the furious tiger managed to flip Baloo over his head. The bear hit the ground with a huge crash.

Suddenly, a lightning bolt struck a
nearby tree which burst into flames.
Shere Khan was terrified! Fire was
the only thing that frightened him.
Mowgli picked up a burning branch.

The Man-cub tied the burning branch to the tiger's tail. Shere Khan screamed as he clawed the branch away. Then he fled into the jungle—never to be seen again.

Mowgli ran over to Baloo, who was lying very still on the ground. "Please get up, Baloo!" he cried.

Bagheera came over to comfort Mowgli. "Baloo was *very* brave," the panther said. "*Was?*" gulped Mowgli. "You mean…?"

Before Bagheera had a chance to reply, Baloo sat up and rubbed his eyes. He was perfectly fine after all! Mowgli laughed and threw his arms around the big bear's neck.

A short time later, the three friends
saw the Man-village on the other
side of the river. Suddenly, they
heard someone singing.

Mowgli peered through the trees and
saw a young girl kneeling by the river.

"Isn't she pretty!" cried Mowgli,
rushing off to have a closer look.

The girl turned and smiled. Mowgli
shyly smiled back. When she began
to walk off towards the Man-village,
Mowgli ran to join her.

Baloo and Bagheera felt very sad
that their young friend was leaving.
But they knew he would now be
happy and safe.

"It's where he belongs," sighed
Bagheera. "Come on Baloo, let's get
back to where *we* belong."

And as the sun set, the two friends
headed back towards the jungle,
singing and dancing happily.